Tales to Tell

Playdate

Scott Wynne

Dark Imagination Entertainment

Author – [Scott Wynne]

Illustrations by [Juaquin Guerra]

[First] edition [2025]

ISBN [979-8-9996916-0-6]

Contents

While my literary compass typically orients itself toward the heroic, the futuristic, or the fantastical—and certainly steers clear of the macabre—this story stands as a heartfelt homage. It is dedicated to **Dennis Comer**, whose profound appreciation for and love of horror was both remarkable and deeply inspiring. By naming a key character *Dennis*, I hope to honor his memory and ensure that his passion for the genre lives on. May it inspire future generations who dare to venture into the dark, the disturbing, and the unforgettable depths of horror fiction.

Introduction

This is the beginning of the publishing works from Dark Imagination Entertainment. This is the first book in a newly released anthology series Tales to Tell. We at Dark Imagination Entertainment hope that you enjoy the Tale we are about to Tell you. Enjoy!

Chapter 1

Funny Biz Pizzeria

Eastport, North Carolina - Funny Biz Pizzeria - October 12th, 2024 11:00 AM

The scent of stale grease—a permanent fixture of Funny Biz Pizzeria—hit Dennis first as he pushed through the front door. Above him, the jangling chime, usually a cheerful announcement, now felt like a blaring alarm, echoing his late arrival through the quiet restaurant. Barely a moment later, Chuck, the owner, rounded the corner from the kitchen. He was a short, barrel-chested man, his thinning hair a mere fuzz around his ears, and his face, usually a roadmap of various anxieties, was currently set in its familiar agitated grimace. A half-smoked cigarette dangled from his lips, its faint wisp of smoke adding another layer to the pizzeria's already complex aroma.

The restaurant was warmer than the crisp fall air outside. The storm, expected later today, was already causing temperatures to drop, and Dennis just wanted to get through his shift before it got bad. The warmer temperature, however, was nothing compared to the intense gaze coming from Chuck.

Chuck mocked, "Late again. I honestly don't understand why I continue keeping you around. You are aware that preparation is required before opening!"

Dennis quickly tied an apron around his slender frame and placed a red work visor over his jet-black hair. The bright red of the visor and dark green apron accentuated his pale complexion. As he prepared, he scanned the pizzeria to see who else was on shift.

Dennis replied sarcastically, "Yes, Chuck, I know. I'm sorry—I had to drop a friend off on my way here. I also know that smoking is not allowed inside."

Annoyed by the comment, Chuck walked

over and shoved Dennis with his robust belly. "You got something to say, wise guy?"

Cowering from the confrontation, Dennis mumbled, "No, sir."

The pizzeria was a basic pizza diner—except for Funny Biz's clown theme. Clown decorations were scattered throughout the building. Despite its intended cheerful atmosphere, the interior had a uniquely depressing feel. The dining area was an explosion of red-and-white checkered tablecloths draped over sturdy wooden tables, each scarred with the faint etchings of countless pizza cutters. Sunlight, usually streaming through the large front windows, typically illuminated framed photographs of old Italian towns and sepia-toned pictures of the original founders—a smiling couple whose legacy was etched into every brick. Today, however, the windows allowed only a minimal amount of sunlight through the overcast sky.

A large wall-mounted television, usually tuned to sports, hummed softly with the local news tracking the storm.

Behind the counter stood a large brick oven—the heart of the kitchen—its yawning mouth a constant source of heat and glowing embers. Stainless steel prep tables gleamed under the harsh fluorescent lights, often dusted with flour and scattered toppings: vibrant green bell peppers, crimson pepperoni slices, and mounds of freshly grated mozzarella. Above, industrial shelves held towering stacks of pizza boxes, ready for the evening rush. The air here was always thick with the sharp tang of tomato sauce and the yeasty sweetness of rising dough—a symphony of smells that spoke of authentic Italian comfort food.

As a few more employees came from the kitchen to start the day's workflow, Chuck—cigarette still in his mouth—headed to his office to put on the pizzeria's clown mascot costume. Dennis turned as a coworker approached. They were about the same age, but that's where the similarities ended.

"Hey Julian, sorry I'm running behind. Hopefully Chuck didn't take it out on you guys," Dennis said.

"Chuck is an old racist, and I'm Mexican—he's always taking shit out on me. But for what it's worth, he's in an extra bad mood because of the party at the nursing home tonight," Julian explained.

"I honestly didn't think he'd go through with the booking, with the storm rolling in," blurted Dennis.

"Greed is a powerful motivator, my friend," Julian said, walking back toward the kitchen.

The door chime rang again, signaling the first customer of the day. A middle-aged man with sandy blond hair and a silver hoop earring, dressed in an orange polo and blue denim jeans, stepped through the door.

Julian walked up to the counter, welcoming the customer. "Right on time, as always, Mr. Abe. Assuming you want the calzones per usual—we already have the order made and ready to go!"

The man smiled kindly and nodded in approval. "Thank you kindly. I'm in a rush to get back to the shop. I had a most unusual package left at the door this morning."

Julian exchanged the food for money. "Anything good?" he asked inquisitively, noticing the excitement on the man's face.

Abe chuckled. "I'm unsure as of right now, to be frank. But I'm optimistic."

"Good luck with it, hombre," Julian said, waving as the gentleman left.

With the short exchange concluded, the man exited the pizzeria. He climbed into his black

SUV and started the engine as Dennis watched through the window. Dennis was familiar with Abe. Since starting three months ago, he had watched him enter at opening every day, ordering the same thing for lunch without fail. Today, however, marked the first time he'd seen him genuinely excited.

Dennis continued working, preparing for what would surely be a long night leading up to the nursing home's giant birthday party.

NNY
BIZ
PIZZERIA

Chapter 2
Killer Sales

Family First Pawn-(Outside)-October 12th, 2024-12:00 PM

Abe pulled into the parking lot of his family's pawn shop, admiring the historic mid-sized building, which seemed as old as the town of Eastport itself. He sat in the SUV, engine idling, as the chill in the air lashed at the vehicle with each gust of wind. Glancing out the window at the leafless trees, he found himself wondering how many years he had left, having recently turned 40 and cursed with terrible genetics.

A spark of excitement shot through him as he remembered the package mysteriously left at the shop door earlier that morning. Abe had opened it before heading out for lunch. Inside the box was a puppet he hadn't seen in an exceedingly long time. It was a character from a children's TV series called *Fuzzy Friends Play Zone*. The show was abruptly canceled after the host went insane, murdered his female co-star, and then committed suicide. To Abe's knowledge, no toys were ever produced due to the incident—so the puppet had to be a prop piece, albeit one that had clearly seen better days.

"Just a quick trip," Abe muttered to himself, rubbing his knees as he shut off the SUV. A familiar ache throbbed in his joints—a testament to years of bustling about. Taking a deep breath, he stepped out, calzones in hand, and moved toward the shop with the briskness his body still allowed. As his hand reached for the door, a sudden, unsettling dread washed over him. He shook his head, pushing the feeling aside, and went inside.

Crossing the threshold, Abe immediately sensed a tension in the air. The place felt heavier somehow. Dust lingered thick in the atmosphere, the particles visible in fractured beams of sunlight streaming through the open door. The windows were fogged with moisture and grime, making it difficult to see outside. He didn't remember them being so dirty when he left that morning.

On the right side of the shop sat tarnished silver such silverware, dinner trays, and the like—while the left side was cluttered with tables heaped with old tools. A massive grandfather clock stood in the far corner, across from the locked jewelry cases, and a few long rifles hung solemnly on the walls.

"Jessie?" Abe called out, referring to his assistant who ran the shop during his absences.

She emerged from the back, her movements almost timid, her eyes darting nervously around the cluttered space. Abe held up their lunch—a brown paper bag from the pizzeria—but he could tell something was off.

"Are you okay, Jess? You look like you've seen a ghost," he said with a chuckle, softening his voice with concern.

Jessie looked at Abe, clearly shaken. "It's just... I've had this eerie feeling ever since that package arrived. The puppet looks bad enough, but Abe... the whole atmosphere feels different. I'm spiritual enough to know when something's off."

"I'm sure you'll feel better after you eat, dear. It's just your nerves. The history behind that puppet is dark—no one can deny that—but if it's truly a prop from the actual show, it could be worth a fortune. It might even be one of a kind." Abe set the food on the counter.

"You're probably right, Abe. It's just that... in my forty years on this earth, I've never had a feeling like this," Jessie replied.

At that moment, the grandfather clock let out a loud chime, startling both Jessie and Abe.

The grandfather clock wouldn't stop chiming, its relentless toll echoing through the shop as if the mechanism had broken. After Abe set the bag on the counter, he then made his way to the clock, fiddling with the mechanisms in the back until the deafening chimes finally ceased.

Still crouched behind the clock, Abe suddenly heard a sound—a loud, wet crunch.

"What was that?" he asked, trying to push himself back to his feet.

When he stepped past the clock, he froze, staring in horror, utterly unable to process what he was seeing. He wanted to scream, but no sound would leave his lips; he was in pure shock. Jessie was making a sound—more of a desperate gurgle than a cry. She still sat on the stool by the counter, an old hatchet lodged deep in her skull, blood streaming down her face.

Jessie finally succumbed to the blow, collapsing lifelessly to the floor.

Then Abe saw it. **Could this have been the culprit?** He continued to stare at the twisted puppet, now standing freely on the counter. To Abe's horror, the puppet let out a slow, malicious grin.

The puppet jumped off the counter and landed on the floor—only to slip in the growing pool of blood.

"Motherfucker!" it rasped in a coarse voice.

Getting to his feet, the puppet began yanking the hatchet from Jessie's skull, spraying blood across himself with every tug.

Abe, tripping, screamed as he fell and crawled backward, scrambling towards the back of the shop. He darted into the bathroom and slammed the door shut, locking it before collapsing into the corner. His hands trembled as he fumbled for his phone. He had to call the police.

Still shaking from Jessie's brutal murder, Abe's fingers struggled to press the right numbers. Then came the sound—the unmistakable

chopping against the bathroom door.

"Oh God," he whispered, eyes wide with terror as pieces of the door began to give way.

Finally, the call went through.

"911, what is the location of your emergency?"

Abe screamed into the phone, voice ragged with panic. "This is Family First Pawn! My assistant's been murdered, and the killer is trying to get to me now! Please, you have to help! He's a black puppet—he has a zipper for a face!"

Just then, Abe looked up. The puppet was crawling through the hole at the bottom of the door, a maniacal laugh echoing in the small bathroom.

"The name is Mr. Zip," the puppet said.

Mr. Zip retrieved the hatchet from the door. He stepped toward Abe, who remained slumped in terror, still gripping the phone.

With a sudden swing, the hatchet buried itself into Abe's hand, pinning it to the wall. Abe let out a bloodcurdling scream. He ripped his arm away, only to realize his hand had been completely severed.

He watched, helpless, as Mr. Zip picked up the dismembered hand—still clutching the phone—and tossed both into the toilet.

Still screaming, Abe tried to crawl away. Blood gushed from the stump where his hand had been. He looked up at the puppet, who stared back with eerie calm.

Then, without warning, Mr. Zip lunged. In an unholy sprint, he crossed the room and began hacking at Abe's neck, striking again and again—until the head came free.

Mr. Zip emerged from the bathroom, carrying Abe's severed head, and moved toward the front door, stepping casually past Jessie's body.

"Prices weren't the only thing slashed here today," he cackled, placing the head in the front window.

He paused, admiring his gruesome work. His sharp eyes spotted the address on the receipt stapled to the brown pizzeria bag.

"Hmm... pizza does sound good," he mused, glancing back at the severed head in the window.

911

Chapter 3
Quality Service

Funny Biz Pizzeria-October 12th, 2024-5:30 PM

Dennis pulled a pizza out of the oven in the kitchen while listening to the TV in the dining area. The dining area itself was empty, as all the customers were ordering pizza for delivery in anticipation of the storm. Dennis placed the pizza in a box, cut it, and stacked it with the others destined for the nursing home delivery—when the TV program was abruptly interrupted by an emergency broadcast.

"We are receiving confirmed reports of a horrifying incident unfolding at Family First Pawn on Maple Street. Authorities are on the scene, confirming multiple fatalities. This is an active and extremely fluid situation. Police are advising residents to remain indoors, shelter in place, and avoid opening doors to strangers.

Details are still scarce, but what we can confirm is that a significant tragedy has occurred, and the individual responsible remains at large.

The victims' last words gave the impression that the suspect may be wearing a mask with a zipper mouth. We'll bring you more information as it becomes available. But for now, the warning remains: stay indoors—this is an incredibly dangerous situation."

Wiping his hands on his apron, Dennis walked into the dining area just as the news reported multiple murders at Family First Pawn. Julian, sitting at a table, watched the television in disbelief. They made eye contact, unsure of what to say.

Julian stood and managed to stutter, "H-hopefully they get that son of a bitch if he hurt Abe."

"Hopefully," Dennis mumbled to himself as he stared blankly at the TV. His gaze remained fixed on the screen, a distant, almost nervous look in his eyes.

Julian looked at Dennis with a concerned expression. "You okay, amigo?" he asked in a joking tone.

Dennis regained his composure. "Yeah, sorry, man," he said. "My nerves are getting to me." He glanced at his watch. "Fuck, I'm running late. I need to take these pizzas to the nursing home. Don't want to ruin this guy's birthday party—at their age, it could be their last," he joked sarcastically.

Julian watched as Dennis emerged from the kitchen, a towering stack of pizza boxes cradled in his arms, and exited through the back door. Dennis quickly arranged the pizzas inside the delivery van. The old engine sputtered to life, and he pulled out of the parking lot just as the first heavy drops of rain began to drum against the windshield, rapidly escalating into a downpour.

Julian stepped to the front door and flipped

the "Open" sign to "Closed." With the day's last order fulfilled, he turned and made his way back toward the kitchen, already anticipating the nightly ritual of cleaning. He reached for the faucet, turning on the water until a steady stream gushed into the large industrial sink.

"Oh, joy. Dishes," he muttered to himself with a weary sigh.

The rain hammered down—a relentless downpour that drowned out every other sound within the pizzeria. But the familiar chime of the front door, faint yet distinct, alerted Julian that he had a visitor. Still scrubbing dishes, he didn't bother to turn around.

"Sorry, we closed early," he called out, his voice straining to be heard over the drumming rain against the roof. "With the storm and all."

A raspy, almost sinister, childlike voice responded, **"I'm really craving Mexican pizza."**

Julian spun around, an annoyed expression

on his face.

"I said we're closed! What part of that didn't you comprehend?" His voice echoed in the empty space.

Confusion then clouded his face—there was no one there.

Julian dried his hands on a towel as he walked toward the dining area. He expected the customer to be there—not the unsettling quiet. But something caught his attention on the door. It was still securely shut. Yet, smeared across the lower pane of glass—at the height of a small child—was a stark, crimson handprint.

His breath hitched.

It looked exactly like blood.

A choked whisper escaped Julian's lips. "What the hell..."

The words had barely formed before a surge of raw panic propelled him to shout, his voice cracking, "Dennis! If this is your idea of a joke, it isn't funny, man!"

The silence that followed was a heavy, suffocating weight.

Instinctively, Julian began backing away, step by slow step, toward the kitchen. Yet his eyes refused to leave the glass door, fixated on the bloody print that screamed of impossible things. The unnerving quiet—thick and heavy—suddenly shattered.

A flush.

The sound, so utterly ordinary, ripped through the silence like a knife.

Julian's head whipped toward the restrooms, a new wave of terror chilling him to the bone.

It came out—a grotesque impossibility torn from a nightmare. A walking felt puppet, lurching forward, its red button eye glinting with horrifying malevolence. A zipper stitched across its face stretched into the most terrifying grin.

The moment its gaze locked on Julian, he was enveloped by overwhelming dread—so tangible it felt like a crushing weight pressing down on his chest.

The puppet began to shamble forward, its button eye never straying from him. A scratchy voice, oddly cheerful for the horror it embodied, rasped, "Oops, my bad! The sign clearly said all employees must wash their hands, and well..."

It paused, the zipper grin stretching wider. "I'm absolutely famished. And I've just been craving something *authentically Mexican*—and you look authentic."

It took another lurching step.

With those words, Julian spun, raw fear overriding every thought, and launched himself into a dead run for the kitchen. Each pounding footstep was a desperate prayer toward the back door—his only escape.

It's got tiny legs, he told himself, clinging to

hope. *There's no way it can keep up. No way at all.*

But a glance over his shoulder shattered that hope.

It wasn't just fast—it was impossible. The puppet was a black blur in his peripheral vision, moving not like a physical being but like a shifting shadow.

One moment, it was on the counter—a gleam of stolen steel in its tiny hand—as Julian's fingers brushed the back door's cold handle. The next, a sharp, excruciating pinch tore through his spine.

His legs buckled.

He crumpled to the floor—awake, every nerve screaming—but utterly paralyzed. He could only watch as the zipper-mouthed horror loomed over him, the knife now poised.

Mr. Zip's grotesque grin widened, an obscene parody of a smile.

"My sincerest apologies for your sudden

spine injury. Truly," the voice rasped, utterly devoid of sincerity. "But I simply can't have you leave before the *main course*."

With a predatory gleam in its eye, Mr. Zip reached down, effortlessly rolling Julian's un-resisting body. It removed his nametag, fingers lingering.

"Ah, Julian. A pleasure to make your ac-quaintance, indeed," it mused, the grin deepen-ing into something truly wicked.

Julian lay trapped—a prisoner in his own skin.

Tears, hot and uncontrollable, streamed down his face, blurring the horrifying image looming above. Every part of him screamed, but no sound escaped. The terror was a living thing, clawing at his throat—a cold, suffocating blan-ket of dread promising an agonizing end.

Chapter 4

Police Brutality

Funny Biz Pizzeria-October 12th, 2024-6:00 PM

Officer Miller pulled his cruiser into the Funny Biz Pizzeria parking lot and killed the engine. It was a long shot, but the receipt stapled to Abe's lunch bag showed this to be his last known location. Camera footage might reveal someone with him—or following him.

As he approached the door, shielding his face from the rain, he saw the **Closed** sign and let out a small sigh. "Another dead end for the day, I reckon," he mumbled. "Well, there's always tomorrow, I s'pose."

He clicked on his radio. "Dispatch, this is Miller. Funny Biz looks like they closed up shop early, prob'ly 'cause of this here storm. I'm headin' on back to the station."

A voice crackled in response, but the storm was causing heavy interference. Just as he turned to leave, he spotted a small, bloody handprint smeared near the bottom of the door.

Miller tried his radio again, but it was no use—only static crackled back at him.

He pushed the pizzeria door open, surprised it wasn't locked, and his hand instinctively went to the grip of his gun. A killer was on the loose, and Miller had no idea what waited for him inside.

A strange yet familiar scent hit him—the unmistakable aroma of baking pizza. Odd, considering the place was supposed to be closed.

Overcast sunlight—what little there was—bled through the windows. A chill snaked down his spine, and Miller drew his weapon.

"Anyone in here? This here's Officer Miller with the Eastport Police Department!" he called out, his voice cutting through the stillness.

A soft, unsettling rustle lured him deeper into the pizzeria, guiding him toward the kitchen.

"I repeat, this here's the police!" he barked again, flicking on his flashlight. The beam cut through the darkness, illuminating the oven area. Just as he gained a clearer view, the floor betrayed him.

His foot slid.

A sharp crack echoed as his head struck the ground. The flashlight bounced, then rolled beyond his reach.

As Miller regained his senses, his gaze fell upon his hand—slick with blood.

Was it him?

The thought barely had time to form before a gleam from the fallen flashlight shone back toward him, revealing the chilling truth: he had slipped in a puddle of blood.

Panic rising, his eyes darted around the shadowed space, searching—until they locked onto a figure in the corner.

His face twisted, a silent scream building in

his throat, as he met the unblinking, red button eye of a hideous creature.

Then he saw it—the gruesome pile beside it.

A sickening jumble of human limbs—arms and legs, grotesquely familiar—stacked in grim display.

Realizing his gun was still in hand, Miller raised it and fired.

The creature moved with unnatural speed, especially for something the size of a child—a blur in the dim light.

Miller's voice ripped through the silence. "What in the actual hell *are* you?"

Mr. Zip's voice dropped to a chilling whisper that seemed to slither through the air. "Truth be told, lawman, you're lookin' at an imp straight outta Hell.

And you're not just gonna *see* what I am, no sir...

You're gonna *feel* it.

Every last bit of your courage's about to curdle, and by the time I'm done… you'll be *beggin'* for the sweet release of true darkness."

A response was the last thing Miller anticipated—much less one that chilled his blood solid. He wasn't the kind to dabble in theology or believe in ghosts and ghouls. Yet, as the creature's sinister words lingered in the air, a terrifying conviction took root deep within him. He knew, with a bone-deep certainty he couldn't deny, that it was telling the truth. And that truth was a horrifying, inescapable weight.

Before the full horror of his situation could even settle, the creature struck.

A blur of unnatural speed in the suffocating darkness, it launched itself at Miller, inflicting deep, brutal cuts with chilling precision. Each gash was accompanied by a high, gleeful laugh—a sound that began to unravel his sanity, stitch by agonizing stitch. Hope withered with every slice, replaced by a suffocating certainty of inevitable defeat.

Mr. Zip's voice dropped to a low, feral growl, dripping with deranged delight.

"These playdates? They're the absolute highlight of my day, lawman. And my imagination—bless its dark heart—is positively bursting with ideas. I'm beside myself with excitement, contemplating just how spectacularly I'll extinguish you. The fascinating agony of dismemberment, limb by bloody limb? Or the exquisite torment of swallowing piping hot grease? Why, the very thought makes me giddy!"

A moment of tense silence followed. Then, a final bang erupted from Miller's pistol before his body went limp.

Mr. Zip's voice oozed disdain in a mock-sympathetic tone.

"A pig, yes, I knew that much. But a coward? Good heavens, you just spoiled all the good bits! I was looking forward to seeing how much longer you'd squeal."

Ding! The oven alarm blared.

Mr. Zip clapped his hands in childlike glee.

"Julian's ready! I mean, the pizza," he corrected with a wide, unsettling grin.

Like a twisted ritual, Mr. Zip carefully added Julian's fingers and peeled face as toppings to the pizza, which already had his innards baked in. He made his way to the dining area and placed the pizza on the table, his eyes gleaming with predatory amusement. Julian's face stared back—a silent, pleading caricature etched into melted cheese.

"Oh, don't give me that look, my dear Julian," Mr. Zip purred, his voice a low, chilling murmur as he brandished the pizza cutter. "You're going to be absolutely divine."

He sliced into the pizza with flair, pulling a

piece free and taking a bite. His eyes closed in perverse ecstasy.

"Simply divine," he rasped, a chilling chuckle escaping him. "Even I underestimated my own artistry. Truly a masterpiece."

A sudden, jarring ring from the phone made him flinch. His features twisted into a scowl at the interruption.

Crossing the room, he cleared his throat before answering. And then, with disturbing precision, he mimicked Julian's voice perfectly:

"Funny Biz Pizzeria. I'm sorry to inform you, we've already closed for the evening. We're a little short-staffed at the moment."

"Hey Julian, it's Dennis. I just got lost and turned around. Could you tell me that address for the nursing home again, please? It's on the counter. I thought I knew where I was going, but I guess not."

Mr. Zip paused, scanning the counter for the

address slip.

"Yeah, man, it's 5150 Village Road."

The words had barely left Mr. Zip's lips before the call abruptly cut out—lost to dead cell service.

"My, my, the universe truly does conspire to bring me joy," he mused, a disturbing grin spreading across his face. "What a convenient turn of events for my next, shall we say... acquaintance."

He snagged a generous slice of Julian pizza for the road, humming softly as he walked toward the door, the storm howling in anticipation.

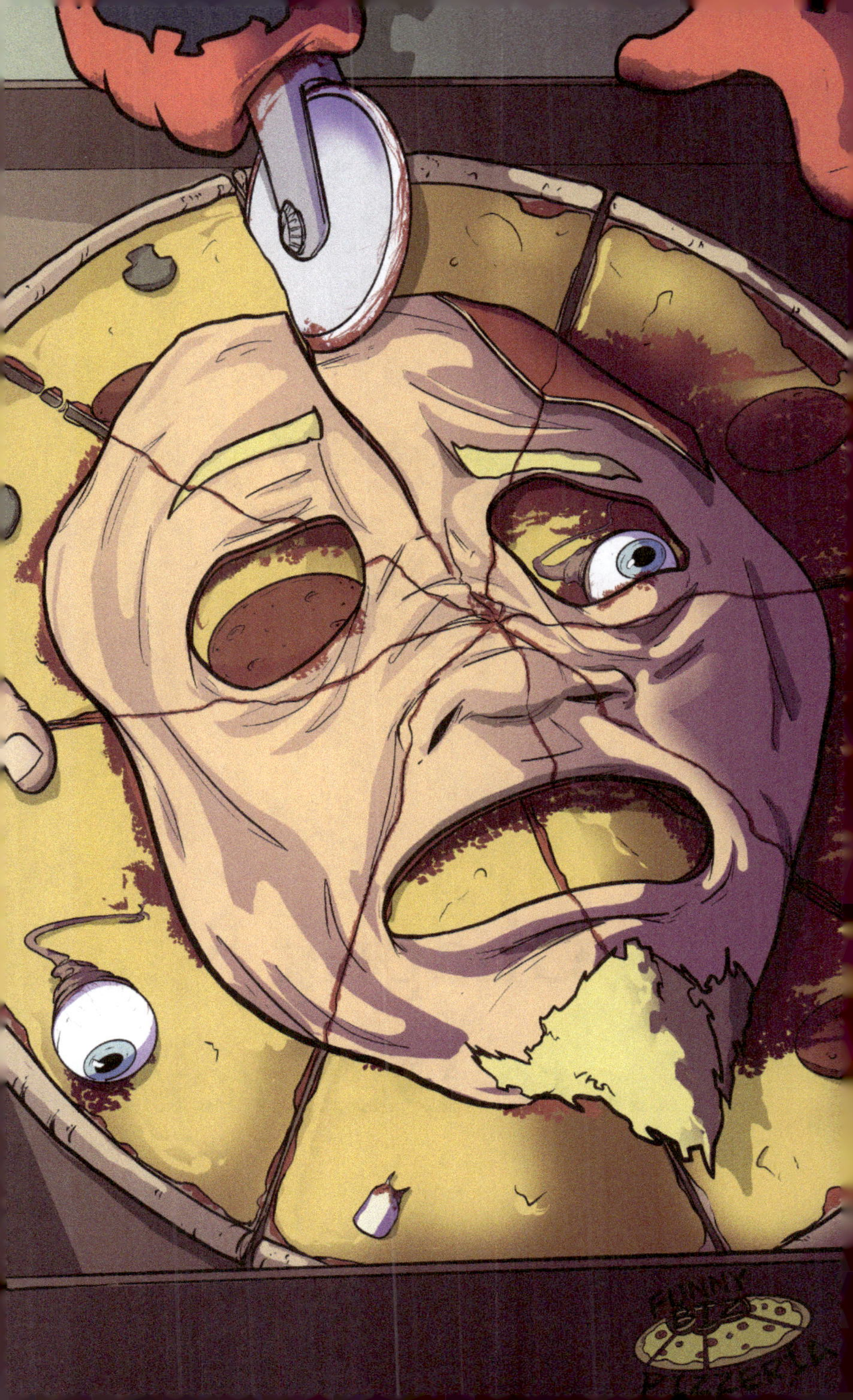

FUNNY BIZ
PIZZERIA

Chapter 5
Late Delivery

Eastport Gardens Senior Center-October 12th, 2024=6:30 PM

Dennis pulled into the Eastport Gardens Senior Center's parking lot. Outside, the storm raged—sheets of rain fell so heavily that visibility was nearly zero. Through the blurry veil of water, the senior center emerged: an imposing, expansive structure of dark brick and countless windows, its sheer size made even more formidable by the relentless downpour.

He had finally arrived, far later than planned—but at least he'd made it. Gathering the pizzas quickly, Dennis dashed through the rain, careful not to let the boxes get soaked. As he stepped inside, shaking off excess water, an agitated orderly approached from behind the front desk, his eyes narrowing in displeasure at the puddle forming beneath Dennis's feet.

The spacious lobby opened up in a welcoming glow beneath warm overhead lighting. To the left, a grand staircase curved upward with quiet elegance. Beneath its rise, the polished tile floor gleamed. To the right, the reception desk was carved from stone that shimmered with subtle flecks of color. In the distance, a door at the end of the central hallway appeared to lead to an outdoor courtyard. Dennis was still taking in the lobby when the orderly's voice snapped him back to reality.

The man was of considerable girth, his starched uniform pulling taut around his middle. His flushed face and the bead of sweat tracing down his temple revealed a simmering agitation. "You're late," he snapped, eyes flicking to the growing puddle at Dennis's feet. "Follow me—if you're done soaking the place."

Clutching the pizzas tightly, Dennis followed the heavy-set orderly, a knot forming in his stomach. Chuck was going to be furious.

The orderly led him into a brightly lit recreation room. It was spacious, lined with rows of activity tables, a small stage at one end, and board games scattered across side tables. Elderly residents and several staff members mingled around the room. At the front, dressed in full clown costume, was Chuck—entertaining the crowd.

The moment Chuck spotted Dennis, his expression darkened. His brows furrowed into a stormy scowl. Dennis hoped to drop the pizzas off quickly and leave before Chuck could confront him. He hurried to the table where the birthday cake was set, dropped the boxes, and turned around—only to find himself nose-to-nose with Chuck, who was now towering over him, arms crossed, a vein throbbing visibly on his temple.

"Chuck," Dennis stammered, his voice rising slightly, "I—I left early and everything! I just got turned around and completely lost in the storm."

Chuck stepped closer, invading Dennis's space, his sour breath hot and heavy with each word. "You're fucking useless, Dennis! This was supposed to be easy money—and now, because you were late, the pizza's gotta be on the house. That's coming out of your paycheck!" he snapped, jabbing a finger into Dennis's chest.

Dennis, defeated, gave a quiet nod and backed away. He turned and slowly headed back toward the doorway he had entered. Before stepping out, he cast one last glance at Chuck—already slipping back into his cheerful clown persona."Fuck you, Chuck," Dennis muttered under his breath.

Making his way briskly toward the entrance, Dennis noticed the storm was still going strong as he passed each window. Then, something caught his eye—a door ajar. He stopped and peeked inside.

An elderly man sat in a wheelchair, staring directly at him. The man had sparse gray hair on the sides of his head, his skin marked by deep wrinkles and sagging lines that revealed every bit of his eight decades. Yet his eyes—his eyes were piercingly clear, holding a startling intensity.

Feeling a strange sense of kinship, Dennis stepped into the room, closing the door behind him with a soft click. He sat down on the bed, the mattress letting out a faint sigh beneath his weight. A heavy silence settled over the small space, the kind that pressed in from all sides. Dennis waited, unsure if the older man would speak first—or if the burden of breaking the silence would fall to him.

The elderly man met Dennis's eyes. "I used to be like you," he rasped, a knowing shimmer in his gaze. "It's the eyes. They always give a person away."

Dennis stared back, a wave of confusion washing over him. He had no idea what was about to unfold, but the man's words stirred something deeper—unease curling like a cold tendril in his chest. That intense gaze, those cryptic words—*"It's the eyes."* What connection did this frail stranger believe they shared?

A knot formed in Dennis's stomach. Apprehension mingled with a reluctant curiosity as he waited, unsure whether to press or retreat.

"Well, old-timer," Dennis said with a nervous chuckle, trying to lighten the mood, "are you going to keep me in suspense, or are you going to explain what that cryptic message is supposed to mean?"

The old man didn't respond immediately. He simply held Dennis's gaze for a long moment—unblinking—before slowly shifting his eyes toward the closet. He raised a trembling hand and pointed.

Dennis stood and walked over. He opened the closet door slowly.

Inside, in the corner on the floor, sat a small wooden chest. A faded lock secured it, and the surface was carved with worn symbols—sigils, maybe. Dennis crouched, examining it.

"I'm sorry," he said, glancing back. "I don't really understand. Do you want me to open this?"

The old man pulled a necklace from beneath his shirt. A small key dangled from it. He removed it with care, holding it in his palm for a long moment as if it bore some great weight. Then, without a word, he tossed it to Dennis—like a man finally shedding a burden too long carried.

Dennis caught the key, knelt again, and unlocked the chest.

Inside was a collection of weathered photographs, old trinkets, and yellowing newspaper clippings. Many clippings referenced a children's television show called *Fuzzy Friends Play Zone*. But scattered among them were articles about murders and disappearances—all occurring around the same time the show aired. One document, near the top, stood out: a discharge paper from the Eastport Sanitarium.

Dennis closed the chest slowly, the weight of what he had just uncovered settling over him. A collection of memories—or trophies? He wasn't sure what they represented to the man behind him. But it chilled him.

He lifted the chest and placed it on the bed, then turned to face the old man again.

"What's your name, by the way?" Dennis asked.

Chapter 6
Road Rage

Funny Biz Parking Lot-October 12th, 2024-6:30 PM

Mr. Zip dragged the severed lower half of Officer Miller to the squad car. With a gruesome effort, he opened the driver's side door and propped the torso onto the seat, carefully positioning the lifeless legs near the pedals and tossing his bloodied knife into the passenger seat. Then, in a truly demented act, Mr. Zip climbed onto the upper half of Miller's body, using it like a grotesque booster seat to gain the height needed to see over the steering wheel. The officer's lifeless legs, now manipulated by Mr. Zip's movements, served as macabre extensions to reach the accelerator and brake pedals.

He keyed the radio, mimicking Officer Miller's voice with chilling accuracy. "Officer Miller checking in. I'll be out and about—no need to check in. The storm's interfering with the radio signal."

Glancing down at the mutilated remains, he chuckled darkly. "Well, at least he's still got his driving legs," he quipped. "I guess you could say he's really *half* the man he used to be."

Mr. Zip pulled out of the parking lot with a jerky motion, making it immediately clear the ride ahead would be anything but smooth. The downpour outside did little to help—the storm had reduced visibility to near zero. Once he merged onto the main highway, at least the rain kept most drivers off the road.

He sped well above the 55 MPH limit, swerving carelessly until he blatantly ran a red light. With a deafening screech of tires and a sickening crunch of metal, the squad car T-boned an SUV. The impact was so violent that Mr. Zip was hurled clean through his windshield. He bounced off the SUV's hood, shattered its windshield, and landed in the backseat.

Several minutes passed before the SUV's driver—a woman in her late thirties with short brown hair—began to stir. A groan escaped her lips as she regained consciousness. A swelling bruise was already forming on her forehead where she had struck the steering wheel. Rain poured in through the shattered glass as she unbuckled her seatbelt, still unaware of the twisted figure silently slumped behind her.

Mr. Zip sat propped in the backseat, a seething storm of malice and fury barely contained. His single button eye glowed faintly, locked on the back of her head. Her lack of awareness only fueled his rage.

The vehicle's Bluetooth chimed, and the screen lit up with the word *Wife*. The driver answered the call.

"Katie, I'm okay," she said, her voice shaky. "I just got into a wreck. I'm about to check on the other driver."

She climbed out and walked to the wrecked

squad car. When she opened the door and saw the remains of Officer Miller, she screamed and stumbled backward in horror. Shocked speechless, she rushed back to her vehicle, her wife's voice echoing over the phone.

"What's wrong? What happened? Tiffany—talk to me!"

But Tiffany couldn't find the words.

"For fuck's sake," Mr. Zip snarled, suddenly springing onto the back of the headrest. His button eye flared as he grabbed the seatbelt, yanking it free and expertly looping it around Tiffany's neck.

He pulled with brutal force. Her hands shot to her throat, clawing desperately at the tightening strap. Mr. Zip leaned in close, his breath cold against her ear.

"Don't take this personally," he whispered, his voice low and venomous, "but if I didn't kill you, it'd kinda make me homophobic. And I'm an *equal-opportunity* kind of puppet!"

He erupted into manic laughter, pulling the belt tighter.

On the phone, Katie's voice cracked with panic. "Tiffany? What's happening? Talk to me!"

But Tiffany could only manage a strangled gurgle before her body went limp.

"Tiffany can't talk right now—she's all choked up," Mr. Zip said with cruel amusement, then ended the call.

Hopping out of the SUV, Mr. Zip made his way back to the squad car. Despite the damage, the vehicle was still drivable. He climbed inside, restarted the engine with a lurch, and peeled away from the wreckage—heading once more toward the nursing home.

Chapter 7

Nursing Home Massacre

Eastport Gardens Senior Center-October 12th, 2024-7:45 PM

The squad car squealed to a halt in the nursing home parking lot, its rattling engine sputtering out. As the driver's door creaked open, the maniacal puppet hopped out, knife in hand, and slammed the door shut with such force that the front bumper clattered to the ground.

Between the heavy rainfall and the impenetrable darkness of night, Mr. Zip moved with chilling speed toward the front entrance. Unseen and unheard, his deathly intent crept like a predator's shadow—silent and unknown to those within—as he slipped unnoticed through the front door.

The same heavyset orderly who had earlier greeted Dennis was still stationed at the reception desk. He was picking his nose, examining the result with a puzzled look, as if genuinely considering whether to eat it. He opted instead to wipe it on his pant leg, missing the brief flicker of movement on the security monitor—movement that showed something approaching the building.

The door opened and closed, but no one appeared to enter.

The orderly rose and ambled over. "Must've been a gust of wind," he muttered, peering out into the storm. Seeing nothing, he shrugged and returned to his desk.

As he sat back down, he caught sight of a faint, zipper-like grin reflected in the monitor. Before he could turn around, a steel blade punched through his temple. Mr. Zip slid the knife free with ease, like cutting through softened butter. The orderly's lifeless body slumped forward onto the desk.

"Well, that's one less person to weigh me

down," the puppet quipped, hopping off the chair and vanishing deeper into the building.

Farther down a sterile hallway, another orderly—older but fit, with neatly trimmed salt-and-pepper hair—pushed a cart filled with medication trays. He whistled a tuneless melody, trying to drown out the crashing storm outside. Oblivious to the growing terror creeping behind him, he continued down the hall.

Lightning flashed outside, casting flickering shadows through the narrow corridor, twisting the sterile white walls into ghostly canvas.

From a darkened room, a pair of red eyes gleamed.

Mr. Zip watched, his button eye locked on the orderly. A wicked grin spread across his face. The puppet slinked closer, mimicking the man's whistling with eerie precision. The orderly paused, brow furrowed, glancing around in confusion.

"Hello?" he called out softly, the storm swallowing his voice.

Without warning, Mr. Zip burst from the shadows, charging at the man with supernatural speed. His butcher knife gleamed under the hallway lights.

The orderly barely had time to react before the blade was sliding into his throat. He stumbled back, eyes wide in terror, hands flying to the wound as blood sprayed across the tile. A strangled gurgle escaped his lips—his scream drowned in his own blood.

Mr. Zip stood over him, watching with a twisted joy. Then, with sudden, frenzied fury, the puppet plunged the knife into the man's chest again and again. Each strike was deliberate, almost playful in its violence.

When he was finally satisfied, Mr. Zip withdrew the blade and wiped it clean on the orderly's blood-soaked jacket. He surveyed his handiwork, admiring the carnage. The body lay splayed out, limbs askew, surrounded by a pool of crimson—a grotesque canvas of sadism and death.

The puppet let out a maniacal laugh, shrill and echoing down the corridor.

He had claimed another victim.

And his bloodlust burned brighter than ever.

A force of pure evil unleashed, Mr. Zip moved forward with deadly purpose. He wouldn't stop—not until the entire nursing home was filled with screams, and his name was carved into the walls of every survivor's night-mares.

A near-cackling sound startled Dennis, snapping him out of the room. Down the hall, a nightmarish scene unfurled—like something ripped straight from the worst horror film imaginable. An orderly lay dead in a pool of blood, his lifeless body crumpled in a crimson-splattered hallway. Standing over him was a black creature with a single, gleaming button eye. It looked up and locked eyes with Dennis.

Then it laughed.

Dennis froze, his stomach turning to ice. The puppet's laughter echoed off the sterile walls, sharp and unnatural. Dennis slowly backed away, one foot at a time, retreating into the room he had just exited.

The older resident—frail and trembling—looked up as Dennis re-entered. His eyes widened with a terror so profound it seemed to age him further in an instant.

"You... you hear that cackle?" he rasped, his voice cracked and weak as a series of wet coughs wracked his chest. "That hellish presence... is it him?"

His gaze drifted toward the doorway.

There, framed in shadow, stood the puppet.

Its zipper-grin curled wider as it stepped

into the dim light.

The old man began to weep, choking on his own saliva. There was no fight left in him. Only dread. He knew—deep in the marrow of his bones—that there was no hope now. His end had come.

The puppet approached slowly, savoring every tremble of fear radiating from the man. The scent of dread was intoxicating, like the aroma of a gourmet meal to a ravenous chef.

"If it isn't my old pal, Russell Thompson, in the saggy flesh," the puppet growled, his voice thick with malicious delight.

Russell's tears flowed freely now. "How.. . how did you know I was here?"

"I always knew, silly boy," Mr. Zip hissed, each word sharp and venomous. "I told you death wouldn't take you—I would. The day you summoned me, the day you stitched me into this puppet body and thought you could control me—I *promised* I'd be the one to drag you back to Hell."

Mr. Zip clenched his knife tighter as he advanced.

"You're the reason I'm here. The reason this whole little blood-soaked game is happening in this town. I felt your life sputtering out like a dying candle, and I figured—why let Father Time have all the fun?" He scoffed, sneering.

"Fear is like wine," the puppet continued, climbing onto the old man's lap, his felt limbs eerily gentle. "And you've been marinating in it for decades. Your soul's gonna be *delicious.*"

The old man's eyes darted to Dennis, frantic and pleading. "Please," he whispered, trembling. "You can still stop him. For the love of God, *save me!*"

In that moment, Russell Thompson's life began to flash before his eyes—an overwhelming torrent of memories, secrets, and sins. He remembered it all: the blood ritual, the desperate invocation, the cursed binding spell that had trapped a hellish entity inside a child's puppet.

Now, with his knife poised above Russell's chest, Mr. Zip gazed into the old man's eyes. Within them, he saw every piece of Russell's twisted history flicker like an old reel of film. Scene by scene. Crime by crime.

The puppet watched with gluttonous glee as Russell relived every horrifying decision that had led to this moment. There was no mercy in Mr. Zip's stare—only cruel satisfaction.

This was his final act. A killing decades in the making.

And it would be nothing short of spectacular.

HE TRIED TO DROWN OUT THE RAGING STORM OUTSIDE WITH A CHEERFUL MELODY.
BUT IN THE SHADOWS, A SINISTER PRESENCE LURKED.

MR. ZIP, WITH HIS GROTESQUE SMILE, SET HIS SIGHTS ON HIS NEXT VICTIM.
E APPROACHED, IMITATING THE ORDERLY'S WHISTLE WITH A CHILLING PARODY.
WHAT WAS THAT?

HE LOOKED AROUND, SEARCHING FOR THE SOURCE OF THE DISTURBING SOUND.
THAT'S WHEN MR. ZIP ATTACK
¡NO!

THE BLOOD SPURTS OUT AS TERROR GRIPS HIM.
HE TRIED TO SCREAM, BUT ONLY A GURGLE ESCAPED HIS LIPS.

Chapter 8

Past Sins

Many years ago-(Part 1)-House in New York City

During a dog-sitting stint, eighteen-year-old Russell Thompson pilfered a children's television prop from his aunt's room. She was a co-host of the whimsical kids' show *Fuzzy Friends Play Zone*. He then carefully placed the puppet inside a meticulously drawn ritualistic pentagram, surrounded by several friends who, like him, dabbled in the occult. Though the puppet was meant to be a vessel for something otherworldly, for Russell and his friend John, the entire elaborate setup was just a joke designed to terrify their unsuspecting friend, Katie.

Russell, John, and Katie—each eighteen—were the kind of inseparable trio you often find teetering on the edge of adulthood, still clinging to the last remnants of their youth. Russell, with his perpetually curious mind, was the unofficial leader, always diving headfirst into the strange and unexplained—a trait that often led them into bizarre predicaments. He had a nervous energy that revealed itself in quick gestures and a constant inability to sit still.

John, the group's resident trickster, was a whirlwind of mischievous grins and sharp wit. He had a knack for harmless pranks and injected playful chaos into their lives, always finding humor in even the most mundane moments. He would feign exasperation at Russell's wild theories but was often the first to encourage pushing boundaries.

Then there was Katie—the pragmatic, sharp-witted one—who acted as the group's moral compass and voice of reason. Fiercely loyal and quick with a sarcastic quip, she concealed a deep well of concern for her friends beneath her tough exterior.

Russell grabbed the book of rituals he'd found at a dusty used bookstore several blocks away and began to chant. His voice deepened, the words rolling off his tongue with chilling intent: "O Dark One, we beseech thee! Bless us with a shadow of your might, an unholy disciple from the deepest pits of Hell, to walk this mortal plane and seek out a most... perfect friend."

Katie reached for the puppet. "This isn't funny, Russell," she said, trying to remove it—but John held her back.

Katie struggled against him. "Katie," he laughed, "the puppet's gonna get you!"

Still smirking, Russell continued his mock-chanting. "With this sacrificial act, we beseech you, O Dark Lord—give this puppet life!"

At that instant, Katie broke free, shoving John away. He stumbled backward—his head striking the sharp corner of the table with a sickening thud. Katie rushed to him, eyes wide with panic.

"Oh God, Russell, get over here! John's really hurt!" she cried.

Russell ran to John's side, frantically checking him. "Oh God, Katie," he gasped. "I think he's dead."

Suddenly, John's eyes shot open. He gasped, clutching the back of his head. "Holy shit, that hurts!" he groaned. "Can one of you drive me to the emergency room, please?"

Katie helped him up. "Yeah, John, you really scared us for a minute."

"You guys go ahead and get him checked out. I'll clean this place before my aunt gets home. She's going to kill me when she sees all this blood," Russell said, glancing around the living room.

Then he noticed something odd.

The blood had formed a thin, winding strea

m... flowing directly toward the pentagram.

With a trembling hand, Russell knelt down and ran his finger through the crimson trail. A chill colder than the air conditioning crept down his spine. Had it moved? Out of the corner of his eye, he could've sworn the puppet—still perched silently in the center—had shifted.

His breath hitched. Every nerve screamed in protest as he stared at the motionless figure. The silence thickened, heavy and oppressive, amplifying the frantic drum of his heart.

It remained still.

But the sensation of unseen eyes watching him refused to leave.

"I could've sworn you were laying down before," Russell muttered, inching closer.

As he reached for the puppet, a grotesque parody of a hand shot out, mirroring his movement. Its once-lifeless features began to twist and contort, reshaping into something monstrous.

Russell recoiled, stumbling back. "Holy shit!" he shouted.

"Oh, don't look so shocked," the puppet rasped, its voice grinding like a rusted hinge in the stillness. It slowly, deliberately rose to its feet. "You're the one who practically sent me an engraved invitation. Honestly—the nerve of some people. Perform a ritual, and then act surprised when the guest of honor shows up."

Russell stared, a cocktail of disgust and awe churning within him. "I mean, I did," he stammered, his voice laced with a newfound uncertainty that shook his perception of reality. "But this kind of shit isn't real."

"Because it didn't fit your perception of reality?" the puppet asked, its voice dripping with mocking condescension. "You made a pact with Hell, and it answered in kind. It's very much a real place—and now, you have its taint on your soul."

"What do you mean?" Russell asked, his voice tight with growing dread. "What exactly does that mean?"

"It means," the puppet began, choosing its words with unnerving precision, "That you are bound to me in, shall we say, a dark friendship that transcends the very bounds of Hell. We now share a responsibility to each other—an almost verbal contract, if you will."

The puppet strolled over to the fridge and swung it open without effort. "One that comes with conditions," it declared, scanning the contents with disinterest. "Such as: I need to feed. And what you'd consider normal food won't satisfy me."

Its gaze drifted from the fridge to the golden retriever, peacefully asleep in its dog bed.

Russell followed the creature's stare, his heart dropping as it locked onto Benny—his aunt's beloved dog, her fur baby, her whole world since she could never have children.

"Are you suggesting eating my aunt's fucking dog?" he shouted, outrage and disbelief twisting his face.

"You see," the puppet said, voice now a silky thread of menace, "my diet consists of human flesh—or something living that can experience real fear. The more suffering their death causes, the better. It's part of the supernatural charm of my presence here, you understand."

It paused, eyes glinting as they scanned the room. "Your aunt's dog will sate me for a while. And her grief when she finds him missing? That will keep me full long after the flesh is gone."

Russell stiffened. "And what happens if I refuse? If I stop you?"

"Well, to make it simple," the puppet said, pulling a knife from the drawer, "I'll gut you like a fish. And make no mistake—if I'm killed or banished back to Hell, you come with me, prince charming. As I said, we're bound now."

Then the puppet began making its way toward the dog.

Russell's new, horrifying reality sank its teeth into him. He wanted to scream, to object, to say anything—but no words came. He could only watch, frozen in place, as the deranged puppet approached Benny, still blissfully unaware in his bed.

The puppet's hand, unnervingly human-like, reached down and gently lifted the dog's head.

Russell's stomach twisted. He squeezed his eyes shut, turned away—and then came the yelp. A single, piercing cry that sliced through the silence, followed by a stillness so complete it echoed in his bones.

The puppet moved fluidly back to him, its steps unnervingly smooth.

"The name is Zip," it said, extending a small,

blood-slicked palm. "Mr. Zip, by the way."

It shook Russell's trembling hand with a grip that made his skin crawl—the warmth of the fresh kill still clinging to it, leaving a damp, crimson smear on Russell's fingers.

Hot, stinging tears finally broke free. Russell stumbled back, unable to take his eyes off the silent horror that had just unfolded. The metallic taste of fear filled his mouth, mingling with the phantom scent of blood.

What in God's name was he going to tell his aunt about Benny—her everything?

The thought twisted his gut. There was no explaining this. No words that could ever make sense of the loss, or of the monster now sharing his reality.

He thought of John and Katie—of telling them. But how could he? Who would believe a story like this?

A living puppet. A blood sacrifice. A

soul-bound pact with Hell.

They'd think he'd lost his mind.

Each ragged breath blurred the line between sanity and madness, and the images—of Zips, of Benny, of that blood-streaked handshake—played on a torturous loop in the wreckage of Russell's mind.

Chapter 9
Televised Violence

Many years ago-(Part 2)-New York City-On-Set of Fuzzy Friends Play Zone-(2 weeks after summoning)

The studio lights hummed, glowing vibrantly over the chaotic set of *Fuzzy Friends Play Zone*. It was a wonderland of oversized plush props designed to ignite a child's imagination. At the center stood a towering treehouse, its branches adorned with brightly colored felt leaves and cartoonish, smiling birds. Below it, a winding blue "river" made of rippling fabric snaked across the floor, dotted with oversized lily pads and friendly-looking stuffed frogs. To one side, a "mountain" of soft green cushions invited climbing, while the other boasted a giant red mushroom with a door, hinting at secret adventures within. Every surface exploded with primary colors—reds, blues, yellows, and greens—creating an almost overwhelming sense of playful energy, a stark contrast to the quiet, empty studio.

Into this whimsical chaos stepped Ms. Linda Thompson, her sensible brown business suit and sleek briefcase an amusing anachronism against the backdrop of fluffy clouds and oversized daisies. Her long, straight blonde hair, usually pulled back in meticulous corporate style, seemed to soften slightly in the playful light. She surveyed the set with an almost imperceptible sigh, a faint smile touching her lips. Adjusting the strap of her briefcase—its leather a dull matte against the glittering, sequined rainbow arching over the main performance area—she allowed herself a moment of calm. Only the distant sounds of crew members preparing backstage punctuated the silence. She found herself strangely enjoying the stillness before the storm—the brief respite before the whirlwind of laughter, songs, and the boundless energy of her co-host, the beloved main host of *Fuzzy Friends Play Zone*. She checked the wall clock, wondering when he would finally arrive.

"Linda, my dearest Linda—so sorry, so, so sorry!" a booming voice echoed through the studio, followed by a flurry of motion.

The main host, known to millions as Burt Rainbow, practically bounced onto the set. He was a whirlwind of energy, a man who seemed to have a perpetual twinkle in his eyes and an irrepressible grin. His bright rainbow tuxedo shone under the lights. His face was extraordinarily expressive, capable of conveying a dozen emotions in as many seconds, and his jet black hair seemed to defy gravity, sticking out in playful tufts.

"You need to go over lines or anything? I know it's been hard—your first day back since Benny went missing." He clapped a hand gently on her shoulder, his wide smile softening into a look of genuine concern.

"I'm fine, Burt. I appreciate the concern," she replied, truly grateful for his friendship.

Burt's eyes, still gleaming with energy, dropped to the sleek briefcase in her hand. "Ooh, is *that* it?!" he exclaimed, his voice practically vibrating with excitement. "Did you bring the new puppet for the show today? The old one's already starting to show some serious wear and tear!"

Linda handed him the briefcase, and Burt eagerly set it on a nearby table, flipping open the latches. His usually joyous expression faltered for the first time. A flicker of genuine surprise—almost alarm—crossed his face. He forced a smile as he turned back to Linda, but the usual sparkle in his eyes was gone, replaced by a shadow of unease. A deep, nameless dread crept into his chest.

The puppet was undeniably the same character as the others—a familiar fuzzy friend from *Fuzzy Friends Play Zone*—yet this version felt... off. Sinister, even. Its very presence made his skin crawl.

And as Burt stared down at it, a heavy sense of hopelessness settled over him.

He knew, somehow, he would have to make this work.

"Alright, places, everyone! Burt, Linda, let's get you two in position!" The director's voice boomed across the set, cutting through the sudden, thick silence that had settled around Burt. He and Linda scurried to their marks—a practiced dance they had performed countless times. Yet as Burt took his place, his eyes were irresistibly drawn back to the table where the new puppet sat. It seemed to pulse with a wicked energy, even from a distance.

The bright, cheerful set—usually a source of comfort and joy—now felt like a sinister stage for a nightmare. Horrifying images flashed behind Burt's eyes: not of felt and stuffing, but of blood-soaked fur and gnashing teeth. He saw the puppet, no longer an innocent character, but a hellish, deformed creature, its painted smile twisting into a predatory grin as it tore into something precious. Something innocent. Benny. Linda's beloved dog.

The vibrant colors of *Fuzzy Friends Play Zone* warped around him. The plush props in his peripheral vision morphed into monstrous shapes. He could almost hear Benny's whimpers, could feel the puppet's rough, fabric form dripping with something dark and foul.

Burt's breath hitched. A cold sweat broke across his forehead. He gripped the edge of the table, his knuckles turning white. The director's voice became a distant mumble. Linda's concerned glance blurred past him. None of it mattered. Nothing existed but the puppet. It wasn't just a prop—it was a hungry, grinning entity. A tangible manifestation of unspeakable evil.

"No... no, no," he muttered, barely a whisper. The puppet's eyes—those seemingly innocent buttons—bored into his soul, promising torment that would never end.

With a primal cry that shattered the forced cheer of the set, Burt snapped. He lunged toward the table, a wild scream tearing from his throat, hands outstretched in a desperate attempt to destroy the monstrous thing before it could consume anything else he held dear.

Then—Blackness.

Burt slowly began to stir, the void receding from his mind. He looked down. A wave of nausea hit him.

He was on top of Linda. Her body lay crumpled beneath him—lifeless. Dark fingerprints, his fingerprints, marred her fragile neck.

He raised his gaze, eyes wide with dawning

horror. The cameras were still rolling. Around him, cast members ran in chaotic disarray, their screams echoing through the set. "He killed her! He killed her!"

A cold, suffocating hopelessness swept over him. But in the middle of the chaos and panic, a singular, grim purpose crystallized in Burt's mind. The cameras were still rolling. Every horrifying second was being captured—broadcast live to a stunned public.

With slow, deliberate steps, he walked toward the giant treehouse that stood at the center of the set. Each step was heavier than the last, as if the weight of the puppet's projected images were dragging him down. Still, he climbed. He grabbed an extension cord, its coils clutched tightly in one hand, and began ascending. The bright, soft branches felt almost welcoming beneath his palms, like the show itself was urging him on.

Reaching a sturdy limb, he fashioned the cord into a crude noose. The plastic felt flimsy and surreal in his grip.

"Hell's real, Russell," he said, staring directly into the camera, his voice raw and desperate—a final, chilling declaration to the audience. Then he jumped.

The cord snapped taut. A sickening crack echoed through the studio. The broadcast caught every second of the moment Burt Rainbow's life ended—seared forever into the collective memory of horrified viewers.

Russell could only watch.

Transfixed. Horrified. His jaw hung slack, eyes wide and unblinking as the monstrous scene played out on screen. He was frozen, a statue carved from disbelief, until the feed was finally, abruptly cut—plunging the room into a cold, disorienting silence.

But one image stayed burned into his mind:

The puppet. Still there. Just sitting on the table, leaning casually against the wall. Waiting.

Chapter 10
Welcome Back Pal

Present Day

What felt like an eternity for Russell was, in reality, mere seconds. A chilling weight settled on his shoulder, and he felt the unmistakable presence of Mr. Zip.

"You see, Russell," the puppet whispered, its voice dry and unsettling, slithering into his mind like smoke, "I've been savoring this for so long. The ultimate game of tag. I was always going to claim your soul."

Mr. Zip's voice grew thick with perverse satisfaction. "All the grief and mourning from that day... all those sad little children because their show ended... all the misery—it kept me sated for so long. I've had my fun in between, to be sure. But the exquisite fear of *you* knowing I was still out there, lurking, waiting... it's been like aging a fine wine. And now, Russell, it's time for vintage. It's your soul."

Russell's wide, terrified eyes dropped from the puppet's malevolent glare to a horrific sight—Mr. Zip was holding his head. His *own* severed head.

A sob tore from Russell's throat. He couldn't comprehend what was happening. He was alive—wasn't he? And yet... he was undeniably dead. The agony coursing through him was unbearable, searing through every nerve. He had to be dead, but the pain was so horribly real.

"I know that look, Russell. You're confused. But make no mistake—you're dead. As dead as the rest of them."Mr. Zip turned the severed head to face him, and Russell saw the tormented faces of all the puppet's previous victims reflected in its twisted features.

Then Mr. Zip laughed—an uncontrollable, high-pitched, echoing screech—before tossing the head toward Dennis.

Dennis didn't flinch. He let the grotesque

object roll to the floor, refusing to catch it.

"You still haven't technically caught me yet, you idiot," Dennis growled, kicking the head back at Mr. Zip. The blow knocked the puppet off Russell's limp body, still slumped in the wheelchair.

Dennis bolted.

He sprinted down the hallway, his footsteps echoing off the linoleum. Bursting through the doors into the recreation room, the loud *bang* startled everyone present. Chuck, who had been entertaining the nursing home residents with his usual over-the-top flair, turned at the noise, irritation flashing across his face.

"Really, Dennis?" he began, taking a few steps forward. "What's the—"

Then his words died on his lips. His eyes dropped to Dennis's feet—just behind them, skittering with a grotesque vitality, was the hideous, puppet-like creature: Mr. Zip.

Chuck froze. His anger vanished, replaced by terror.

Unfazed, Dennis strode toward the cake table. His eyes locked onto the cake-cutting knife buried in the white frosting.

"Clowns are double points," he muttered, a grin stretching across his face—too wide, too cold.

The residents watched with morbid curiosity, assuming this was just another strange skit. It wasn't. Before anyone could react, the room exploded into a nightmare.

Dennis struck first.

A blur of motion, he grabbed the knife and drove it into Chuck's chest. Once. Twice. Again. Each plunge was met with a sickening squelch.

Mr. Zip followed, leaping onto Chuck's back. His own blade—a razor sharp, almost surgical-looking thing—sank into flesh. Chuck's screams were cut off as Dennis, with a final, savage thrust, slit through his throat, silencing him.

Gasps and terrified whimpers replaced the laughter.

Dennis wasn't done.

He crouched, grabbed Chuck's limp hand, and began methodically sawing off his fingers. One by one. Each severed digit landed with a soft *plop* on the tile. Then he went for the neck.

With brutal determination, he began sawing, the blade catching on bone and sinew. The sound was unspeakable. Wet. Grating. A slow, deliberate tearing.

Finally, Chuck's head fell free, rolling with a dull thud onto the checkered floor.

Dennis turned and braced himself against the door, locking it.

His breath came fast, wild, as his eyes darted between the stunned residents and the butchery behind him.

Mr. Zip, meanwhile, moved with eerie precision. He delicately gathered Chuck's fingers, one by one, placing them carefully atop the cake like grotesque decorations.

Then, with the flair of a showman, he lifted Chuck's severed head and set it in the center of the cake, its lifeless eyes staring up at the flickering fluorescents.

He even added the severed fingers as candles.

"A cake fit for the King of Hell himself," Mr. Zip chittered, his voice gleeful and mocking, sending a new wave of shivers down Dennis's spine.

With a flourish, he snatched the matchbox from the table and struck a match. One by one, he lit the candles, the flickering flames dancing across the blood-spattered room, casting grotesque shadows against the walls.

And the audience—those poor, elderly

souls—finally understood. They screamed.

Mr. Zip turned, his head cocked at an unnatural angle, just in time to spot Dennis. He wasn't just killing the elderly residents—he was *butchering* them.

Those who could still move, however feebly, were being systematically cut down, their gurgling cries echoing through the once-peaceful recreation room. Blood pooled in lazy rivulets under wheelchairs. Panic painted every surface.

With a joyful hop, Mr. Zip dismounted the table, his small form darting with unnerving speed. He didn't just stand by. No, he became part of the carnage.

He weaved between the wheelchairs, wheeling the remaining immobile residents to the center of the room with eerie cheerfulness. In the heart of that helpless cluster, he began stacking oxygen tanks—one after another—forming a precarious tower of impending doom.

"This will be my *finest* work!" he squealed. "Behold, dear Dennis—the **Geriatric Bomb!**"

His high-pitched cackle scraped against the edges of reality like a rusty saw on bone. He threw his tiny arms wide, as if unveiling a masterpiece to the cosmos, a mad artist delighting in his grotesque exhibit.

The elderly, now a trembling huddle of frailty and confusion, could only whimper and sob. Their bodies twitched with fear, but they had no strength left to flee. They knew. Mr. Zip, efficient and gleeful, opened the valves on the oxygen tanks. A soft *hiss* filled the air—a deadly lullaby. He didn't need to say it; the flickering candles still burning on the grotesque cake would do the rest.

Dennis heard it before he saw it—the rising wail of sirens, distant but drawing closer, cutting through the hiss of escaping gas.

"Someone must've called the cops," he muttered to Mr. Zip, jaw tight. "Let's bail."

Just as they turned to escape, the puppet suddenly skittered back to the cake.

"No way I'm leaving without a piece for the road!" Mr. Zip chirped. He snatched a slice, fingers and all, the severed head of Chuck still crowning the confection like a nightmarish trophy. "A little midnight snack," he added with a wink.

Then, with casual grace, he leapt onto Dennis's shoulders like a grotesque jockey atop his mount, and the two bolted out the back door.

Rain hit their faces—a brief, forgotten sensation—before Dennis picked up speed. His legs pumped with desperation, driving them farther from the inevitable. Farther from the fire.

They didn't stop until they were well down the street, hidden in the shadows of trees and silence. Then they turned.

The blast hit like the hand of a god.

A deep, thunderous *rumble* cracked the air, followed by a sudden flash of blinding light. The nursing home erupted in a violent bloom of fire, a colossal inferno tearing through the night.

Dennis and Mr. Zip stood still, faces bathed in hellish light.

Flames roared into the sky like demon claws. The building's frame buckled and groaned. The explosion wasn't just physical—it *felt* alive, pulsing with dark energy. A fire pit pulled straight from the bowels of Hell.

"That was one wild game of tag," Dennis murmured, his voice raw, his eyes reflecting the inferno's dance. "Let's go home. I'm beat."

Mr. Zip looked down at him, button eye twinkling in the crimson glow.

"You are a sick son of a bitch," he said, oddly affectionate. "I can't believe you actually let me turn those old people into a bomb. Best night *ever!*"

They turned away, leaving the burning building behind. The sirens were fading now, swallowed by the distance and the hiss of dying rain.

Ash settled on their clothes like morbid confetti. Smoke clung to the humid air like a ghost refusing to depart. Streetlights flickered above them, casting long, distorted shadows—monstrous in size and intent.

"So, where to next?" Mr. Zip asked, voice chipper, almost childlike.

Dennis didn't slow his stride.

"You know the rules," he replied, a smile creeping across his face, lit by the fading glow of the fire. "Anywhere and anyone... just no kids. "He patted the puppet's head—a gesture disturbingly gentle. "Let's see what the next town over has. Maybe they've got a snooty mayor.

Or a surprisingly flammable historical society building."

Mr. Zip chuckled as the darkness wrapped around them.

"Oh, by the way—*tag, you're it.*"

Dennis let out a dry laugh.

"I bet you've been waiting to say that since I dropped you off at Abe's this morning."

The two walked on, swallowed by the night.

Chapter 11
After Chapter

Several weeks after the Eastport massacre-Undisclosed Town

When Dennis pulled open the motel room door, the creak seemed to echo through the stale, threadbare gloom of the place. Dust floated lazily in a shaft of light from the flickering neon sign outside. He stepped in and dropped a duffel bag and a battered suitcase onto the sagging mattress; both landed with a dull thump beside an unidentifiable stain that had long since stopped trying to justify its existence.

With a sigh, Dennis unlatched the suitcase.

Mr. Zip popped out, his signature grin stretched wider than usual—wide enough to reveal a set of dazzling, disturbingly pristine teeth.

Dennis recoiled slightly. "Are those... fucking dentures?"

Mr. Zip gave an exaggerated wink, running a

tiny hand over his gleaming new set of chompers.

"Don't tell me you took those back in Eastport," Dennis added, the shock briefly overpowering his usual weariness.

The puppet cackled, teeth clicking with mechanical perfection. "A man's got to keep up appearances, Dennis. And yes—Eastport. Surprisingly good selection for a town that perpetually smelled like despair and discount hot dogs. I even got a two-for-one deal. These beauties"—he gestured proudly at his grin—"and a slightly used kidney."

Dennis snorted, pulling a wrinkled shirt from his duffel bag and tossing it carelessly onto the bed. It landed near the stain. "You know, I was thinking about the day we met," he said. "Seeing you with Russell two weeks ago kinda made me reminisce. Feels like forever ago now."

Mr. Zip didn't look up. "I'll take a rain check

on the sentimentality, pal," he rasped, snatching the TV remote and flipping through channels with manic energy. "New town means new opportunities. I need inspiration if I'm gonna top the *geriatric bomb.*"

His grin twisted again as he plucked out the dentures with a theatrical *pop*, holding them aloft like a trophy.

Dennis rolled his eyes and muttered, "Jesus."

The screen bathed the dim room in flickering light, the static hiss blending with the low hum of the broken air conditioner.

The story continues...

The adventures of Dennis and Mr. Zip will resume in the upcoming novel: ***Mr. Zip: Town of Sin***

www.ingramcontent.com/pod-product-compliance
Lightning Source LLC
Chambersburg PA
CBHW071534100726
47908CB00004B/1392